D0392096

WELCOME TO
PASSPORT TO READING
A beginning reader's ticket to a brand-new world!

Every book in this program is designed to build read-along and read-alone skills, level by level, through engaging and enriching stories. As the reader turns each page, he or she will become more confident with new vocabulary, sight words, and comprehension.

These PASSPORT TO READING levels will help you choose the perfect book for every reader.

READING TOGETHER
Read short words in simple sentence structures together to begin a reader's journey.

READING OUT LOUD
Encourage developing readers to sound out words in more complex stories with simple vocabulary.

READING INDEPENDENTLY
Newly independent readers gain confidence reading more complex sentences with higher word counts.

READY TO READ MORE
Readers prepare for chapter books with fewer illustrations and longer paragraphs.

This book features sight words from the educator-supported Dolch Sight Words List. This encourages the reader to recognize commonly used vocabulary words, increasing reading speed and fluency.

For more information, please visit passporttoreadingbooks.com.

Enjoy the journey!

Little, Brown and Company

Hachette Book Group
1290 Avenue of the Americas, New York, NY 10104
Visit us at lb-kids.com

Little, Brown and Company is a division of Hachette Book Group, Inc.
The Little, Brown name and logo are trademarks of Hachette Book Group, Inc.

The publisher is not responsible for websites (or their content) that are not owned by the publisher.

First Edition: February 2015

Library of Congress Control Number: 2014953726

ISBN 978-0-316-28352-6

10 9 8 7 6 5 4 3 2 1

CW

Printed in the United States of America

Passport to Reading titles are leveled by independent reviewers applying the standards developed by Irene Fountas and Gay Su Pinnell in *Matching Books to Readers: Using Leveled Books in Guided Reading*, Heinemann, 1999.

DISNEY FAIRIES

Tinker Bell

AND THE LEGEND OF THE

NEVERBEAST

Meet Nyx
the Scout Fairy

By Jennifer Fox

Illustrated by the Disney Storybook Art Team

L B

LITTLE, BROWN AND COMPANY
New York • Boston

Attention, Disney Fairies fans!
Look for these words when you read
this book. Can you spot them all?

hawks

rocks

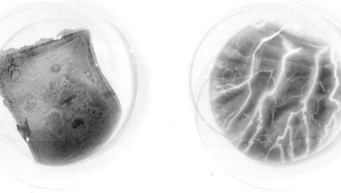

map

lightning

Nyx is the leader
of the scout fairies.
She keeps
Pixie Hollow safe.

Some hawks swoop in!

Nyx and her team are ready.

"Let us handle this!" she says.

Nyx is fast and brave.
She scares the hawks
away from Pixie Hollow.

One day, Nyx hears

a loud roar.

"What was that?" she asks.

Nyx asks the scouts to help her.

They talk to
the fairies and
take notes.

Nyx finds paw prints in the woods.

She stops to look at a plant.

Something took a bite out of it.

The scouts find

some rocks, too!

Nyx goes to the Book Nook
to get more facts.
She finds a map.
It tells the story of
the NeverBeast.

Nyx brings the map to the queen.

Fawn is there, too.

Nyx tells them that

the NeverBeast is coming.

The sky turns green.
A storm is coming.
Nyx and her team fly
fast into the woods.

Fawn flies in with
the NeverBeast.
She tells the fairies that
he collects lightning.

He gathers the lightning
in his horns and wings.
Fawn and the NeverBeast
head into the storm.

Lightning is drawn

to the rock tower.

Nyx is there.

She hits the tower and

makes the lightning scatter.

The NeverBeast falls down.

27

A bolt is about
to hit Nyx.
The NeverBeast
gets up and stops
it just in time.

Nyx is safe.

Next, the beast flies
into the eye of the storm.
The lightning is drawn
to his horns.
The storm is stopped.

The NeverBeast's horns
are burned, but he is safe.
The fairies cheer.
Pixie Hollow is free from danger.

Nyx was wrong about
the big furry beast.
She bows and thanks him
for saving Pixie Hollow.